T0132063

Chicken Jail

Sarah P. Ross

Art by P. Amanda Thomas

To order additional copies of this book, contact:
Xlibris
844-714-8691
www.Xlibris.com
Orders@Xlibris.com

ISBN: Softcover   978-1-6698-7032-6
        EBook   978-1-6698-7031-9

Print information available on the last page

Rev. date: 03/13/2023

2

Why is Fluffy in jail, I ask?
Why is such a sweet chicken in jail?

It all began with baby chicks in a bath,
baby chicks too big for a pail.

We must build a house for our chickens
to sleep. We must build a chicken
coup to stay dry for our peeps!

8

Buffy our chicken is a caramel brown with a butt that fluffs from her petticoat down!

Muffy our chicken is black striped with white! She is the one who stays up late at night.

Fluffy our chicken is white and black speckled. She looks like a fireman's dog with black spots that are freckled!

14

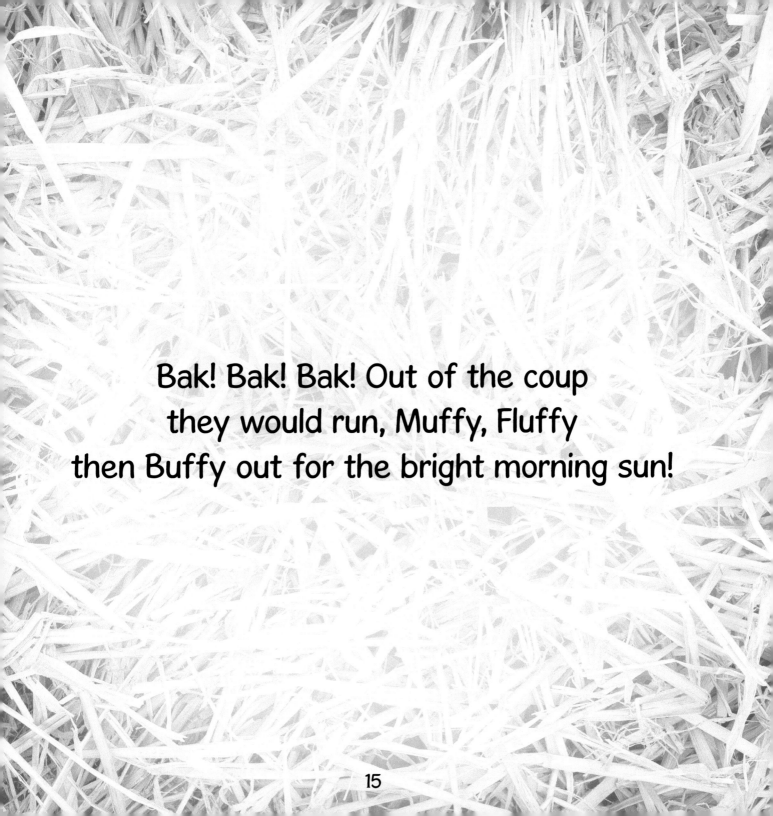

Bak! Bak! Bak! Out of the coup
they would run, Muffy, Fluffy
then Buffy out for the bright morning sun!

Grain and green grass they loved
to peck, then dust in the dirt
all the way to their neck!

One day something bad began! Fluffy started bullying Muffy around their playpen!

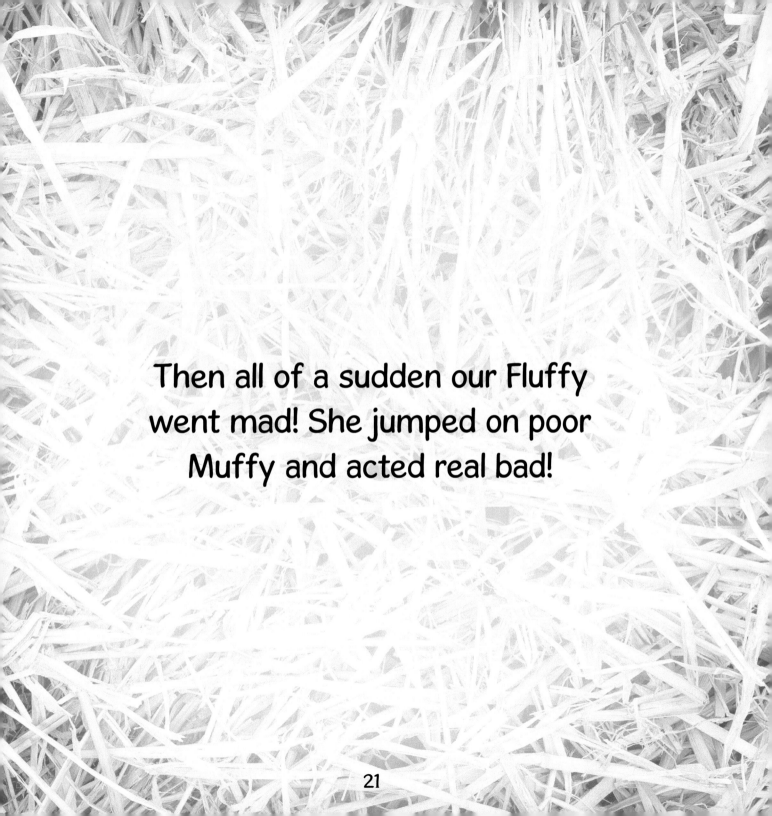

Then all of a sudden our Fluffy went mad! She jumped on poor Muffy and acted real bad!

So we had to put Fluffy in Chicken Jail
to keep her there for only a spell.

At night we would protect our
chickens from the chilling dew
and blanket Fluffy's cage as she would coo!

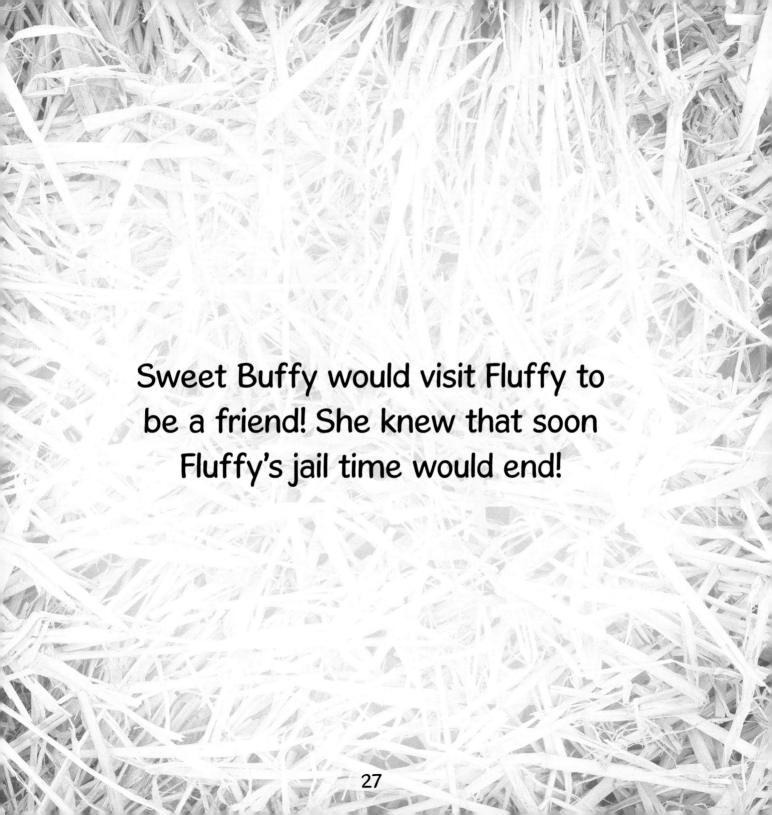

Sweet Buffy would visit Fluffy to be a friend! She knew that soon Fluffy's jail time would end!

We decided it was time to
return Fluffy to the pen
so happy to see all three as good friends!

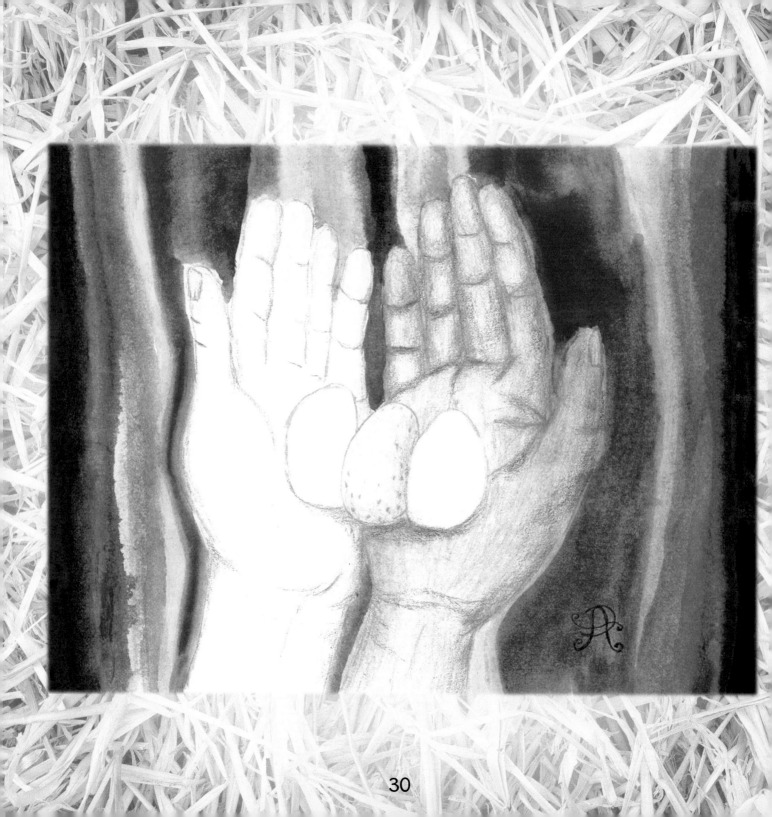

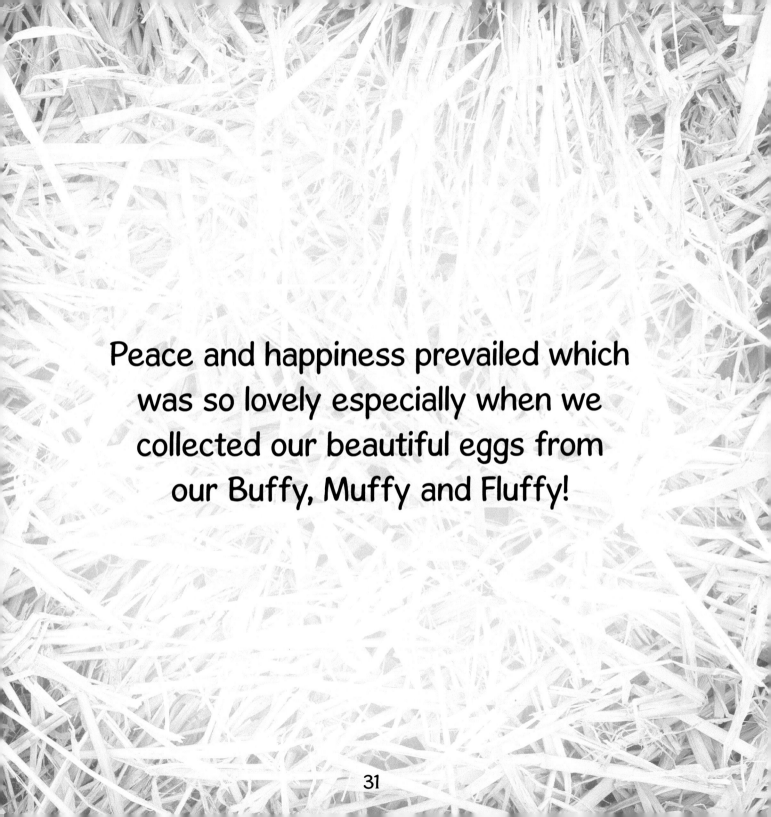

Peace and happiness prevailed which was so lovely especially when we collected our beautiful eggs from our Buffy, Muffy and Fluffy!

Printed in the United States
by Baker & Taylor Publisher Services